BRITAIN'S CANADA
1613~1770

TITLE LIST

BRITAIN'S CANADA
1613-1770

BY
SHEILA NELSON

MASON CREST PUBLISHERS
PHILADELPHIA

Mason Crest Publishers Inc.
370 Reed Road
Broomall, Pennsylvania 19008
(866) MCP-BOOK (toll free)

First printing
1 2 3 4 5 6 7 8 9 10

Library of Congress Cataloging-in-Publication Data

Nelson, Sheila.
  Britain's Canada, 1613–1770 / by Sheila Nelson.
      p. cm. — (How Canada became Canada)
  Includes index.
  ISBN 1-4222-0003-5   ISBN 1-4222-0000-0 (series)
  1. Canada—History—To 1763 (New France)—Juvenile literature. 2. Canada—History—1763–1791—Juvenile literature. 3. Great Britain—Colonies—America—Juvenile literature. I. Title.
  F1030.N323 2006
  971.01—dc22

Produced by Harding House Publishing Service, Inc.
www.hardinghousepages.com
Interior design by MK Bassett-Harvey.
Cover design by Dianne Hodack.
Printed in the Hashemite Kingdom of Jordan.

CONTENTS

INTRODUCTION

by David Bercuson

Every country's history is distinct, and so is Canada's. Although Canada is often said to be a pale imitation of the United States, it has a unique history that has created a modern North American nation on its own path to democracy and social justice. This series explains how that happened.

Canada's history is rooted in its climate, its geography, and in its separate political development. Virtually all of Canada experiences long, dark, and very cold winters with copious amounts of snowfall. Canada also spans several distinct geographic regions, from the rugged western mountain ranges on the Pacific coast to the forested lowlands of the St. Lawrence River Valley and the Atlantic tidewater region.

Canada's regional divisions were complicated by the British conquest of New France at the end of the Seven Years' War in 1763. Although Britain defeated France, the French were far more numerous in Canada than the British. Britain was thus forced to recognize French Canadian rights to their own language, religion, and culture. That recognition is now enshrined in the Canadian Constitution. It has made Canada a democracy that values group rights alongside individual rights, with official French/English bilingualism as a key part of the Canadian character.

During the American Revolution, Canadians chose to stay British. After the Revolution, they provided refuge to tens of thousands of Americans who, for one reason or another, did not follow George Washington, Benjamin Franklin, or the other founders of the United States who broke with Britain.

Democracy in Canada under the British Crown evolved more slowly than it did in the United States. But in the early nineteenth century, slavery was outlawed in the

British Empire, and as a result, also in Canada. Thus Canada never experienced civil war or government-imposed racial segregation.

From these few, brief examples, it is clear that Canada's history differs considerably from that of the United States. And yet today, Canada is a true North American democracy in its own right. Canadians will profit from a better understanding of how their country was shaped—and Americans may learn much about their own country by studying the story of Canada.

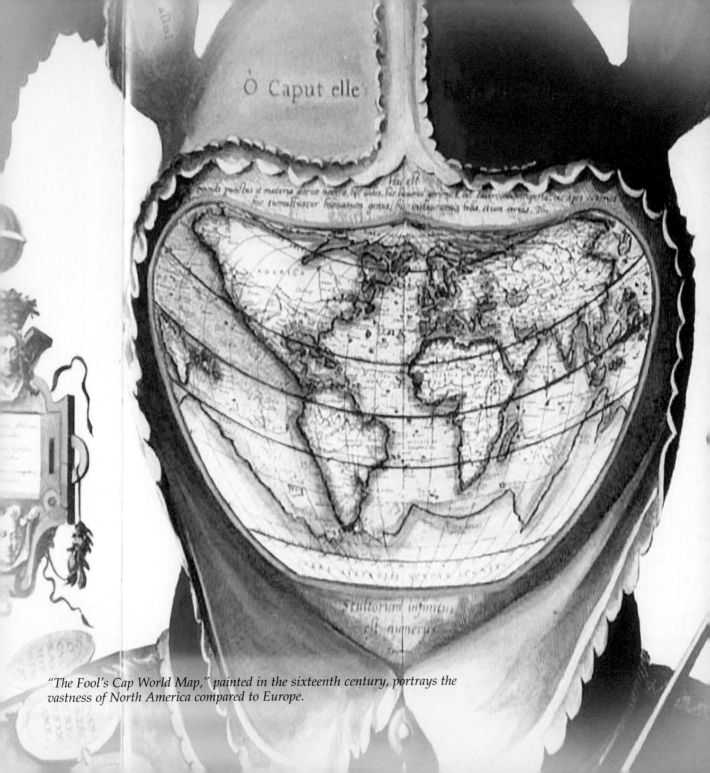

"The Fool's Cap World Map," painted in the sixteenth century, portrays the vastness of North America compared to Europe.

One

CONFLICTS BETWEEN ENGLAND AND FRANCE

The story of the English in early Canadian history is the story of their conflict with the French. Although geographically close, the beginning of the 1600s found England and France far, far apart. They spoke different languages and had different religions. For centuries, England and France had been at war in Europe, with brief times of peace between the fighting.

In the sixteenth century, England and France both claimed land in North America. Although this new land was huge, England and France wanted vast and overlapping expanses of it. For a while, very few European settlers lived in the New World, but gradually more and more people began to make their way across the ocean to build little communities along the coast and inland on the rivers. Before long, the problems England and France faced in Europe began to spill over into their New World colonies.

In 1497, John Cabot claimed the east coast of North America for England. He was the first European to land on the mainland of North America; Columbus had landed in the islands of the Bahamas five years earlier. Cabot's land claims were vague and did not give the exact area he was claiming on behalf of England. Later, England would use the right of discovery to say the entire east coast of North America was its territory. Although John Cabot was Italian (he was born Giovanni Caboto), since he had been

Jacques Cartier

working for England when he discovered North America, the English said, North America belonged to England.

The problem with the right of discovery was that it was hard to enforce. North America's east coast was thousands of miles long, and for many years it was sparsely populated. Nearly a hundred years after Cabot's discovery, England slowly began working to colonize the new land. It built colonies at Jamestown in Virginia in 1607 and on the east coast of Newfoundland at around the same time.

Meanwhile, the French had sent Jacques Cartier to the New World in 1534. Cartier explored the St. Lawrence River and claimed the region for France. In the early 1600s, France founded colonies at Port Royal, along the coast of what is now Nova Scotia, and at Québec, on the St. Lawrence River. France called the area around Port Royal "Acadia" and the area along the St. Lawrence River "Canada." These were both French provinces in the larger New France, an area that covered nearly as much of North America's east coast as the English claims.

Samuel Argall Attacks Acadia

In 1611, the English discovered France had established a colony at Port Royal, an area claimed by the English Virginia Company. Worse, they learned *Jesuit* priests had arrived in Acadia and had started working to convert the *First Nations* people to Roman Catholicism. The Church of England had broken away from the Catholic Church in the 1530s, and ever since, the English had distrusted Catholics.

In 1613, the governing council of the Jamestown colony voted to send Captain Samuel Argall north to check out the

John Cabot sailing from England to the New World

*A **parallel** is an imaginary circle around the earth that measures latitude.*

French colony and to get rid of any French people living in "English" territory, any land south of the forty-sixth **parallel**—an area including Acadia, but not the St. Lawrence River. Argall arrived first at Mount Desert Island, off the coast of Maine, where a group of French Jesuit priests had begun founding a colony only two months earlier. Argall captured the priests and burned their buildings before continuing on to the north.

At Saint Croix Island, where the French had built a short-lived colony in 1604, Argall stopped and burned the remains of the French buildings. He wanted to wipe out all evidence that the French had ever lived in the area.

When Argall arrived in Port Royal, the governor, Jean de Poutrincourt, was in France raising support for the colony. Poutrincourt's son Charles de Biencourt and most of the French were away as well, hunting with the local Mi'kmaq. Argall took the opportunity to loot the settlement, taking

England or Britain?

Did you ever wonder why England and Britain appear to be two names for the same country? Before 1707, the country was called England. In 1707, the parliaments of England and Scotland joined to create the Parliament of Great Britain. After 1707, the country was referred to as Britain.

Great Britain

what he wanted before burning the buildings and crops.

When Poutrincourt returned to Port Royal the next spring, he found his colony in ruins and a group of ragged, starving settlers waiting for him. He took most of the colonists back with him to France, leaving his son to rebuild.

Argall had attacked the French colonies with the authorization of the Virginia Company in Jamestown but without the direct permission of King James I. In England, the authorities conducted an investigation and decided Argall had been right to destroy the French settlements.

New Scotland

Samuel Argall's attacks on French colonies in Acadia had not settled anything; both England and France still believed they owned the area. In 1621, Sir William Alexander, a Scottish nobleman and poet, convinced King James to give him land in

A farming settlement in Nova Scotia

the New World to create a "New Scotland" (in Latin, "Nova Scotia"). Alexander had read a lot about North America and wanted to start his own colony. He thought the best way to encourage the Scottish to become colonists was to give them a place of their own in the New World.

King James granted Alexander all the land between Newfoundland and New England and agreed to give out *titles* to men who wanted to settle in New Scotland. The new *barons* would be responsible for bringing over settlers.

Alexander had trouble finding people who wanted to buy land in New Scotland. He tried to send a small group of settlers to his new colony in 1622, but the ship left late and then ran into bad weather before reaching New Scotland. The colonists spent the winter in St. John's, Newfoundland, and then returned to Europe without ever setting foot in New Scotland.

In 1629, Alexander was finally able to gather a group of settlers to travel to New Scotland. Alexander's oldest son—also named William Alexander—led the party. Near the site of the French Port Royal, Alexander founded a Scottish colony named Fort Charles.

The Scottish discovered quickly that winters were long and harsh in New Scotland. *Scurvy* set in during their first winter at Fort Charles—caused by a lack of vitamin C in their diet, although they did not understand the cause of the disease. Thirty out of the seventy colonists died before spring.

The Kirke Brothers

While Sir William Alexander fought to recruit settlers to establish his New Scotland in French Acadia, others looked to the French colonies in Canada and the fertile land along the St. Lawrence River. In 1627, England went to war against France, and the war quickly spilled over into the New World colonies. In 1628, England's King Charles I sent the five Kirke brothers—David, Lewis, Thomas, John, and James—to North America with orders to drive the French out of Canada.

The Kirkes sailed up the St. Lawrence River to the French colony of Québec and demanded the French surrender. Québec's governor, Samuel de Champlain, refused, and the Kirkes left without having taken the colony.

After this—instead of attacking Québec directly—the Kirkes captured the little French fishing station of Tadoussac, near the mouth of the St. Lawrence, and set up a base there. Before long, a fleet of ships arrived from France, carrying supplies and new

16

England's King Charles I

Titles are terms of honor bestowed on the basis of rank, office, privilege, attainment, or land.

Barons were the lowest level of English nobles.

Scurvy is a disease where the teeth get loose and the skin bleeds.

Great Britain's King James I was far away from what was happening in his New World colonies.

settlers to Québec. As the French entered the river, the Kirkes attacked, seizing the supplies Champlain had been counting on to make it through the winter. Having captured the French supplies, the Kirkes returned to England for the winter. In Québec, the settlers suffered without the food and provisions they had expected to receive from France. In the spring of 1629, the Kirke brothers sailed back to Canada, where the Québec settlers were now starving. This time, Champlain agreed to surrender the colony. The Kirkes rounded up the French and sent them to England as prisoners.

Newfoundland's Placentia Bay

By this time, England and France had made peace, but King Charles did not want to give up the French colonies he had captured.

*The **Parliament** is the British legislative body.*

The French Return to New France

The English held on to their captured French colonies for four years. Back in England, though, King Charles I was having financial problems. England had become involved in several expensive wars, with both France and Spain. The English *Parliament*—who did not fully support King Charles because of his marriage to a Roman Catholic French princess—refused to give Charles the necessary money to fund the wars. The king found himself paying for the English wars out of his own pocket, and that money was quickly disappearing.

By 1632, King Charles was desperate. He made peace with both Spain and France, but also disbanded Parliament. This meant he now had to raise all the money to run the country.

*A **dowry** is the money, goods, or estate a bride brings to her husband or his family in marriage.*

When Charles married the daughter of the king of France in 1626, the French agreed to pay a large **dowry**. Five years later, however, they had paid only part of the agreed amount. Charles badly needed the rest of the money. Finally, through the Treaty of Saint-Germain-en-Laye, Charles agreed to return the New France colonies of Québec and Port Royal to the French, while the French would pay the rest of the money they owed King Charles.

In 1632, the Kirkes left Québec, and the Scottish left their New Scotland. France again had control of New France.

Newfoundland's rocky coast

20

The European colonies of the New World were only decades old, but already England and France had fought several battles over the land. In the years to come, Acadia especially—still claimed by both countries—would become a battlefield in the continuing dispute. For the time being, however, France ruled the northern part of the continent, with the exception of Newfoundland. The island of Newfoundland, although used by many European countries as a fishing station, had been in the hands of England since John Cabot discovered it in 1497. Still, the English had many years of failed Newfoundland colonies ahead of them, as they faced snow and cold and struggled to survive on the rocky coasts.

21

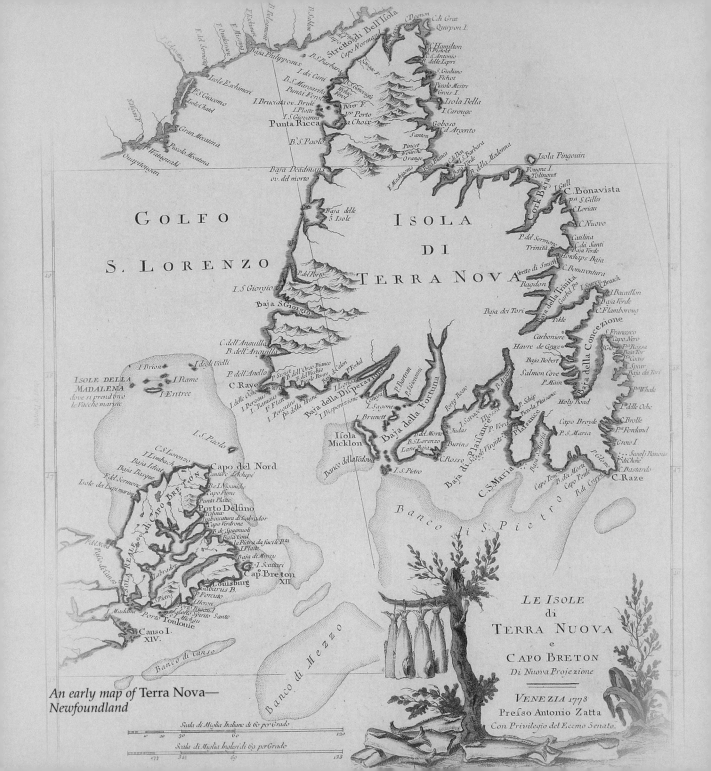

An early map of Terra Nova—Newfoundland

LE ISOLE
di
TERRA NUOVA
e
CAPO BRETON
Di Nuova Proiezione

VENEZIA 1778
Presso Antonio Zatta
Con Privilegio del Eccmo Senato.

Two

THE NEWFOUNDLAND COLONIES

Standing on the shore looking out to sea, John Guy felt satisfied with the colony he had founded the summer before. In August of 1610, Guy had arrived in Cupids, Newfoundland, with thirty-nine colonists. They were sent by the Newfoundland Company to establish a settlement and begin farming, fishing, and exploring the area. The settlers had brought with them a variety of animals—cows and ducks, pigs and hens, rabbits, geese, and goats. Before winter set in, they had built houses and stables to shelter the animals.

The winter was snowy and cold, but not as bad as Guy had feared. Four colonists died, but this was far less than the deaths in the early Virginia colonies. Throughout the winter months, Guy continued exploring and hunting. He already had a collection of furs ready to take back to England in the fall.

The First Official Settlement

John Guy's colony at Cupids—then called Cuper's Cove—was not the first English settlement in Newfoundland, but Guy's colonists had been the first group sent officially from England. In 1583, Sir Humphrey

A modern-day fishing community in Newfoundland

planting crops. Plenty of wildlife could be found inland, and the ocean at their doorstep overflowed with fish. In 1612, Guy brought sixteen women from England to join the colony.

Gilbert had formally claimed Newfoundland for England. Gilbert had intended to plant a colony there himself, but he died in a shipwreck on the return trip to Europe. In the decade before John Guy arrived, families of fishermen had begun to build homes for themselves in the rocky coves of Newfoundland's coast.

At first, Guy was optimistic about the future of Cupids. The settlers had started

Unfortunately, just as things were looking good, the problems started. The shallow, rocky soil would grow a few small vegetables, but no grains at all. Local pirates, such as Peter Easton, sailed from settlement to settlement, raiding communities and kidnapping men. The winter of 1613 was so bad some of the animals died of starvation. The English colonists realized their first three winters had actually been mild. In 1615, John Guy went back to England and resigned as governor of Cupids. His optimism had been broken by his failure to grow crops, by long and terrible winters, and by frequent pirate attacks.

John Mason's map of Newfoundland is an unusual one because it shows south at the top.

Some colonists went back to England with Guy, but most stayed. The Newfoundland Company sent John Mason to replace Guy as governor. Mason had a lot of military experience, and the company felt he could handle pirate attacks better than Guy had done. Mason may have been able to deal with the pirates, but he did not have any experience with fishing; he did not know how to govern a fishing community.

In 1621, Mason moved to New England, and the Newfoundland Company withdrew

St. John's

When European fishermen started spending their summers in Newfoundland in the early 1500s, St. John's harbor quickly became the most popular gathering place. The large harbor was close to the fishing on the Grand Banks and offered shelter during storms. Instead of having been officially settled by a group of colonists, the city grew up gradually as more and more fishermen decided to spend the winters in Newfoundland. Soon, St. John's became a thriving city. Today it is the capital of Newfoundland and is known as the oldest "European" city in North America.

its support from the Cupids colony. Even though the colony had access to an abundance of fish, the company did not realize the kinds of profits it had hoped for.

The settlers began leaving Cupids after Mason's departure, although most of them stayed in Newfoundland. Several groups moved further along the coast and started their own settlements. By 1631, the colony had been abandoned except for a few fishermen who camped there during the summer months.

The Beothuk

When England's King James I authorized John Guy to establish a colony in Newfoundland in 1610, he instructed Guy to find the Native people living on the island, to set up a trade relationship with them, and to convert them to Christianity. For a long time, Guy could not find anyone to trade with or convert, although he knew they existed. Explorers and fishermen had occasionally caught sight of Natives on the

Ocher *is an earthy, red or yellow color, derived from impure iron ore and used as pigment.*

shore. They called them the Red Indians, since they painted their bodies with red *ocher*—but their real name was the Beothuk. Soon, many Europeans started referring to all Native people in North America as "redskins."

In 1612, Guy sailed back and forth along the coast of Newfoundland for a month, looking for some sign of the Beothuk. Even at this early stage, the Beothuk had learned to avoid Europeans; in the early 1500s, explorers had kidnapped dozens of their people and taken them back to Europe. While other First Nations traded with the European newcomers, exchanging furs for metal, the Beothuk discovered they could

John Guy's first encounter with Beothuks

loot abandoned fishing camps for metal goods. In this way they could avoid interacting with Europeans.

At last, after spotting a fire on the shore, Guy was able to approach a little group of Beothuk and trade some goods with them. The Beothuk were cautious at first, but they soon relaxed as they saw Guy did not appear threatening. This was the only friendly encounter between the Beothuk and Europeans in recorded history.

Sometime later, the captain of an English ship passing through the area saw a large group of Beothuk waiting on the shore as he approached. Frightened and thinking the Beothuk planned to attack, the captain fired his cannon over their heads. The Beothuk quickly disappeared and did not try to trade with the Europeans again.

By avoiding Europeans, the Beothuk managed to escape most of the disease epidemics that wiped out huge numbers of First Nations people elsewhere on the continent, but this did not save them in the end. The Beothuk needed the fish and seals from the coasts to survive, but growing numbers of settlers pushed them further and further inland. In the interior of Newfoundland, the Beothuk could hunt caribou and beaver, yet starvation became a constant threat.

Later, when fur trappers invaded the inland forests of the island, the Beothuk had nowhere else to retreat. They stole from the trappers, and in retaliation the trappers often killed any Beothuk they saw. In 1823, a Beothuk girl named Shanawdithit was kidnapped and was able to describe her dying culture in a series of drawings before she died of tuberculosis in 1829. Although many people searched for the Beothuk after this time, no more were ever found. Shanawdithit was the last known Beothuk.

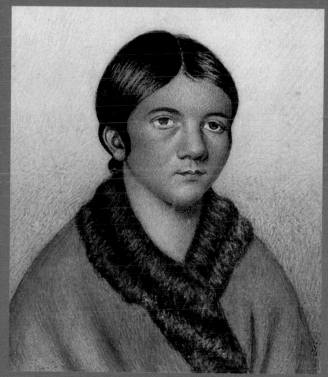

A portrait of Shanawdithit

29

Seventeenth-Century Travel Brochures

To help encourage colonists to travel to North America—a long and dangerous journey across the Atlantic Ocean with more hardships waiting on the other side—landowners would sometimes write books or pamphlets describing their New World lands. Some of these people had never left Europe, such as William Vaughn, a poet who wrote *The Golden Fleece*, an imaginative and not very accurate book about Newfoundland. Others, like Richard Whitbourne, had actually lived in Newfoundland. In 1620, Whitbourne wrote *Discourse and Discovery of Newfoundland*, a much more truthful and detailed book than Vaughn's.

The Avalon Colony

George Calvert served in the court of King James I, but his real interest was in the New World. In 1620, he was able to buy a piece of land in Newfoundland, which he named Avalon after an island paradise in Celtic mythology. The next year, Calvert sent a group of colonists to build a settlement in Avalon. The settlement was called Ferryland, an English version of a Portuguese word for the area. The colony did well at first, since Calvert was wealthy and able to provide his colonists with plenty of food and supplies.

In 1625, Calvert converted to Roman Catholicism and resigned from his official positions in the court. England was a Protestant country, and Catholics were not allowed to serve in important positions. King James liked Calvert, however, so he gave him land in Ireland and made him a baron with the title Lord Baltimore.

Calvert decided to make his Avalon colony a place where all Christians, both Protestants and Catholics, could live and

George Calvert

Calvert had brought two Roman Catholic priests with him to Avalon, and the Protestant minister already living in the colony objected strongly. By spring, Calvert and his wife were fed up with their Avalon colony. Calvert wrote that Newfoundland was a "wofull country" and asked King Charles for some more southern land. In 1632, just after Calvert died, King Charles

Cecil Calvert

worship freely. In 1627, he traveled to Newfoundland for the first time, and the next year he brought over his wife and family to live in the mansion he had built for them.

Soon, though, Calvert realized Avalon was not the ideal place he thought it would be. The winter of 1628–1629 was long and severe, stretching from October to May. England and France were at war, and French pirates attacked the colony repeatedly. Even within the colony, things were not peaceful;

granted his son Cecil Calvert land that would become the U.S. state of Maryland.

Even though the Newfoundland winters were too harsh for Calvert, many of his colonists stayed in Avalon, living and fishing in an area called Ferryland. The colony became one of the oldest permanent English communities in Canada.

The First Governor

In 1628 and 1629, the Kirke brothers, led by David Kirke, captured New France on behalf of England. Even though King Charles had given back the captured land to the French in 1632, he knighted David Kirke in 1633 for his actions. In 1638, Kirke became the first governor of Newfoundland, and the next year he moved into Calvert's mansion in Ferryland.

Up to this point, each settlement had its own governor, but Kirke had authority over all the English communities in Newfoundland. As governor, Kirke built forts, brought a hundred settlers from England, and charged the local fishermen tolls.

A group of merchants, called the Western Adventurers, who had been in control of the Newfoundland fishery, did not like Kirke's authority over them. The Western Adven-

turers did not want any settlers coming to Newfoundland. Official colonies meant government control, and the merchants wanted all the power and control of the fisheries to themselves.

The Western Adventurers accused Kirke of giving the best fishing spots to foreigners and of building taverns. Taverns meant the fishermen drank and did not do as much fishing. Kirke was able to show that the merchants just wanted to get rid of him, however, and he was able to keep his position as governor for a while longer.

In 1651, Cecil Calvert sued David Kirke for taking over the colony of Avalon and the settlement at Ferryland, which had belonged to Cecil's father, George Calvert. When King Charles gave Kirke the land in 1638, he was acting on the idea that Calvert had abandoned Avalon and that it therefore could be freely given away again. By 1651, King Charles was no longer in power in England. He had been beheaded in 1649, after being declared a traitor by Parliament. Oliver Cromwell, as head of Parliament, now ruled England. Kirke was thrown into prison in England, where he died in 1654.

Kirke's wife and sons went back to Newfoundland and settled there permanently. Lady Sara Kirke took over the management of the fishery and became one of the richest fishing merchants in

The Newfoundland Coat of Arms granted to Sir David Kirke in 1638, now the Province of Newfoundland's official seal

Newfoundland. She was possibly the first woman *entrepreneur* in North America.

Although Cecil Calvert eventually regained control of his father's Avalon colony, he never traveled to Newfoundland,

> An *entrepreneur* is someone who assumes the costs and risks of starting or running a business.

33

One of Newfoundland's present-day fishing communities

and life in Avalon went on as it had before. England did not appoint another governor to replace David Kirke, and until the first half of the eighteenth century, no single governor ruled Newfoundland again.

The beginnings of English Newfoundland were unique in North America. Usually, English merchants would form a company and send a group of settlers to build a colony, work the land, and send back profits to England. In Newfoundland, several companies tried this kind of colony—John Guy's colony at Cupids was the first—but the expedition leaders almost always left, complaining of harsh winters and soil incapable of growing crops. The people who stayed were mostly fishermen, strong people used to dealing with hardships.

They certainly faced plenty of hardships in their new lives. Besides the usual dangers of fishing on the open seas, they had to deal with cold, snowy winters, pirate raids, and groups of merchants who did not want them in Newfoundland. Rather than organized colonies, these fishermen built tiny settlements tucked away in sheltered coves.

From only a few seasonal fishermen in the sixteenth century, the population of Europeans in Newfoundland grew to a few thousand permanent residents by the end of the seventeenth century. In the process, the settlers had unknowingly begun leading to the extinction of the Beothuk.

In the mid-1600s, English settlement and control in what would become Canada was limited to the island of Newfoundland. That would soon change. Although the French controlled the huge St. Lawrence River—and therefore the fur trade—the English would soon be given the chance to form their own trading company and to compete with the French.

The islands of the St. Lawrence

Three
THE HUDSON'S BAY COMPANY

Twenty-year-old Pierre-Esprit Radisson sat up straighter in his canoe, dipping his paddle into the St. Lawrence River and steering toward Québec. Ahead of him he could see his brother-in-law Médard Chouart des Groseilliers' canoe. Around them were hundreds more canoes, each paddled by a Cree. Every canoe was filled with beaver pelts. Radisson smiled as he thought of the excitement on the faces of the people when they saw all the furs. He thought of how happy the governor would be and how he would reward Radisson and des Groseilliers.

Canada, which relied on the fur trade to survive, had been having trouble getting furs lately. The Wendat, who had supplied the French with furs for years, had been shattered by wars with the Iroquois. Now, in August of 1660, Québec needed every fur it could get. The furs Radisson and des Groseilliers were bringing would make a huge difference.

As the flotilla of canoes drew closer to the colony, a cannon blast echoed from the fort.

Radisson frowned, wondering what it could mean. A little group stood on the wharf, obviously waiting for them.

"You are under arrest," one man said as they climbed onto the wharf. "You had no trading license to obtain these furs. Your furs will be confiscated and you will be fined."

Radisson could only stare in shock. This was not the welcome he had expected.

Turning to the English

Radisson and des Groseilliers were disgusted at the reception they received on their return to Québec. Their confiscated furs brought a great deal of money into Canada, but they had seen none of it. They had also brought back information on new trade routes, but Québec's governor wanted to keep France's focus on the St. Lawrence region.

In frustration, the explorers turned to the English. They traveled south to Boston and met with representatives of King Charles II. The representatives were very interested in what Radisson and des Groseilliers had to say, especially when they said the English could access fur trade routes through Hudson Bay.

England had been in possession of Hudson Bay since Henry Hudson discovered it in 1610, while searching for a passage

Pierre-Esprit Radisson

Pierre-Esprit Radisson lived a life of adventure from the time he was very young. He was born in France but moved to Québec with his half-sister when he was a little boy. When he was eleven, he was captured in an Iroquois raid and adopted by an Iroquois family. Several years later, he escaped, but he was recaptured and tortured before being taken in again by his adopted family. Later, a Dutch governor offered to buy his freedom, but Radisson refused, choosing instead to escape shortly afterward. After his escape, he traveled throughout the Great Lakes region with his sister's husband, Médard Chouart des Groseilliers. During his life, he had a wide variety of experiences, from taking part in First Nations rituals to talking with the king of England. Radisson valued his freedom and let nothing stand in his way when he wanted to do something.

Radisson and des Groseilliers formed relationships with First Nations groups.

through North America to the Pacific Ocean. Since Hudson Bay clearly did not lead to the Pacific, the English lost interest. The route to reach the bay was far to the north and difficult to navigate for much of the year. The English had seen no economical reason to do anything with Hudson Bay until the two French explorers made their suggestion.

King Charles's representatives arranged for Radisson and des Groseilliers to go to London and speak with the king directly. At first the king was a little skeptical of the stories the explorers told; Radisson especially had a tendency to exaggerate. Prince Rupert, Charles's cousin, was excited about the idea of building a fur trading empire out of Hudson Bay, though, and he convinced the king to finance an exploratory expedition to the region.

Hudson's Bay Company

In 1668, two ships, the *Eaglet* and the *Nonsuch*, left England and headed for Hudson Bay. After a bad storm, the *Eaglet*,

Fur traders

Searching for furs

with Radisson on board, was damaged and had to return to England. The *Nonsuch*, carrying des Groseilliers, went on and sailed south inside Hudson Bay to James Bay. At the south end of James Bay, by the mouth of a river the English named Rupert River, the men built a trading post called Charles Fort and spent the winter there.

In the spring, a group of Cree whom des Groseilliers had been able to contact arrived

*A **monopoly** is when one company either controls an industry or is the only provider of a particular product or service.*

at the fort with loads of furs to trade. The men exchanged goods with the Cree, loaded the furs onto the *Nonsuch*, and went back to England. This was a far easier way to do things than how the French had been trading. While the French sent men in canoes far into the wilderness to negotiate fur trades with First Nations trappers, the English only needed to sail their ships into Hudson Bay and meet the Cree who would bring the furs to them.

Back in England, King Charles was thrilled at the success of the voyage. On May 2, 1670, he granted the Hudson's Bay Company a *monopoly* to trade on Hudson Bay and James Bay and along all the rivers that drained into the bays. Prince Rupert headed the company, and the land included in the royal charter was named Rupert's Land in his honor.

WANTED.

A FEW stout and active YOUNG MEN, for the service of the HUDSON's BAY COMPANY, at their Factories and Settlements in AMERICA. The Wages to be given, will depend on the qualifications of each individual: very good hands may expect from £12. to £15. a year, besides a sufficient allowance of oatmeal, or other food equally good and wholesome. Each person must engage by contract for a period of THREE YEARS, at the end of which, he shall be brought home to Scotland, free of expence, unless he chuses to remain at the Settlements of the Company, where THIRTY ACRES of GOOD LAND will be granted, in *perpetual feu*, to every man who has conducted himself to the satisfaction of his employers. Those who are thus allowed to remain as settlers after the expiration of their service, may have their Families brought over to them by the Company at a moderate freight. Every man who chuses to make an allowance to his relations at home, may have any part of his wages regularly paid to them, *without charge or deduction*. No one will be hired, unless he can bring a satisfactory character for general good conduct, and particularly for honesty and sobriety; and unless he is also capable of enduring fatigue and hardship. Expert Boatmen will receive particular encouragement. Those who are desirous of engaging in this service, will please to specify their names, ages, and places of abode, as also their present station and employments, and may apply to

at

A Hudson Bay Company want ad

The Impact of the Hudson's Bay Company

The presence of the English in Hudson Bay changed the face of Canada. The French did not like the involvement of the English in the fur trade. Many First Nations people found it easier to trade with the English, and as a result the French received fewer furs.

Radisson and des Groseilliers thought the English could easily be getting even more furs. They were frustrated the English chose to do all their trading from Hudson Bay, rather than striking out along the rivers. In 1675, they went back to the French and in 1682 helped them found La Compagnie du Nord to compete with the Hudson's Bay Company. After their first voyage on behalf of the new French company, however, the Québec government again tried to cheat the two explorers out of their fair profits. Des Groseilliers gave up in

The French hated having the English intruding on their territory and their livelihood. In 1686, they sent Pierre de Troyes north through a series of rivers to Hudson Bay. De Troyes and his men attacked the southern English forts on James Bay and captured them. Over the next several years, the English and French fought for control of Hudson Bay, until the Treaty of Utrecht returned the region to Britain in 1713.

Before Pierre-Esprit Radisson and Médard Chouart des Groseilliers arrived with their news about the potential of Hudson Bay for the fur trade, the English had little hope of spreading into the northern parts of North America. The French held the St. Lawrence waterways and controlled the fur trade. The formation of the Hudson's Bay Company allowed the English to consider pushing into the rest of Canada. Soon, wars between England and France in Europe would give England an excuse to try to conquer New France.

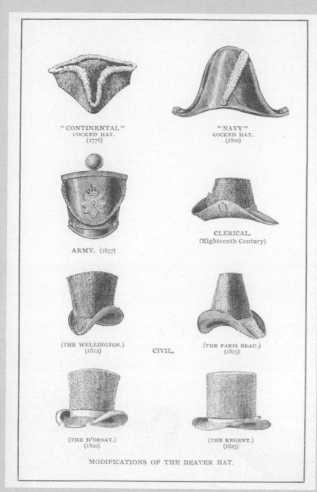

Beaver pelts would be used to make these stylish European hats.

disgust and retired, but Radisson, who was younger, went back to the English and signed on again with the Hudson's Bay Company.

Halifax, Nova Scotia

Four
THE FIGHT FOR ACADIA

Seven English ships sat in the harbor, their cannons pointed at the French settlement of Port Royal. Sir William Phips, the English commander, approached the French colony, a foot soldier next to him holding a white flag high to show they had only come to talk.

The French were outnumbered. Phips had arrived with hundreds of soldiers, while only seventy men, most of them farmers, guarded the settlement. The French governor, Louis-Alexandre des Friches de Meneval, chose not to fight a hopeless battle; when Phips asked for his surrender, he agreed.

King William's War

In 1688, war broke out in Europe, with France on one side and England on the other. A year later, the war arrived in North America—the first in a series of wars that would be known as the French and Indian Wars. In North America, this war was known as King William's War. The French, with their First Nations allies, began attacking English settlements and Iroquois villages, since the Iroquois were allied with the English.

Acadia, France's East Coast territory, offered the easiest target for the English. The French province was sparsely populated

Sir William Phips

maintain the English claim—he needed every soldier he had for the attack on well-fortified Québec. Instead, he took prisoner the French governor, Meneval, the two Jesuit priests in the colony, and the few French soldiers who had been stationed at Port Royal. Then he made the remaining settlers take an oath of loyalty to England. After looting the settlement, he sailed away, leaving the Acadians alone with the wreckage of their homes.

On his way to Québec, Phips looted and destroyed the other French communities along the coast of Acadia. Soon, all of Acadia had fallen into English hands. By the time Phips reached Québec, winter was just around the corner. Phips did not want to get trapped with his ships in the ice of the St. Lawrence River. When he demanded that Frontenac, the French governor, surrender, the response was defiance and the thunder of cannons. After a three-week standoff, Phips left and went home to Boston.

King William's War continued for another three years. During most of the war, Acadia was officially in the hands of the English, although the French settlers remained. The Acadians tried not to get involved in the conflict. They simply wanted to live their lives in peace. In 1697, the Treaty of Ryswick ended the war and returned Acadia to the French.

and geographically separated from Québec. In 1690, the English sent Sir William Phips to take over the Acadian settlements—especially the capital Port Royal—and then to attack Québec itself.

Although Phips easily defeated the French at Port Royal, he could not afford to leave any of his men at the settlement to

Queen Anne's War

The peace between England and France did not last long. In 1702, war began again in Europe, this time over who would become Spain's next king. In Europe, the war was called the War of the Spanish Succession, while in North America it was Queen Anne's War, the second of the French and Indian Wars.

Again the French launched a series of vicious attacks on English settlements, slaughtering settlers and burning towns. In retaliation, the English sent soldiers to attack Acadia once more. This time, however, Port Royal was better defended and remained unconquered through a battery of English attacks. Other Acadian communities, who did not have the defenses of Port Royal, were attacked again and again during

During Queen Anne's War, the French enlisted the help of many First Nations groups.

Plunder *is something stolen by force, especially during war.*

Anglican *means relating to England.*

Annapolis Royal

Fort Anne in Nova Scotia

Queen Anne's War. The English burned Acadian houses and fields and took away loads of *plunder*, although they did not kill the settlers as the attacking French often did.

In 1707, while England fought its wars in both Europe and North America, the Act of Union joined the English and Scottish parliaments to create the Kingdom of Great Britain. Since England and Scotland were now one country, ruled jointly, together they were usually referred to as Britain.

In September of 1710, the British launched another attack on Acadia, concentrating on Port Royal. The Acadians in Port Royal had had a hard year. Their crops had failed, and France had not sent any supplies or reinforcements. By the time the British arrived, they were starving and ragged. Less than three hundred men, many of them only teenagers, guarded the French fort, while the British commander Francis Nicholson attacked with a force of two thousand. In spite of the odds, Port Royal held out for two weeks before surrendering.

Nicholson changed the name of Port Royal to Annapolis Royal, named for Queen Anne. He took prisoner the French soldiers and sent them back to France. Colonel Samuel Vetch stayed in the newly named Annapolis Royal as governor, along with nearly five hundred British soldiers. Port Royal had finally fallen to the British.

Acadia's Golden Age

In 1713, Queen Anne's War ended with the Treaty of Utrecht. The treaty returned Hudson Bay and Newfoundland to the British, while the French kept their St. Lawrence colonies around Québec. Britain also took Acadia, although France kept the islands in the Gulf of St. Lawrence, including Cape Breton Island, which they called Île Royale, and Île St. Jean, which would later become Prince Edward Island.

Even though Britain now governed most of Acadia, the majority of the settlers were still French. They spoke French, and they were mostly Roman Catholics instead of *Anglican* Protestants. They agreed not to attack the British and to stay out of any conflicts between the British and French, but they wanted to be left alone as well. For the most part, the British left the Acadians alone for the next several decades, letting them farm their lands in peace. This was all the Acadians really wanted. This period of peace under British rule became known as the Golden Age of Acadia.

Nova Scotia's fertile wilderness

Acadia's location, between the strength of warring British and French colonies, had not been a comfortable one. As the weakest of the French North American territories, Acadia suffered constant British attacks before the final defeat at Port Royal in 1710.

Although the French Acadians went on to live in an uneasy peace under the British for more than thirty years, the differences in nationality and culture would soon create problems too great to be ignored.

The War Elsewhere

Although the British took Port Royal from the French during Queen Anne's War, the French had taken many of Britain's colonies. In the north, the French had claimed most of the Hudson Bay trading forts. In Newfoundland, Pierre le Moyne de Iberville raided and burned British settlements, capturing them for France.

Nova Scotia's snowy coast

Five
A DIVIDED LAND

"I promise and swear by my Faith as a Christian that I will be entirely faithful and will truly obey His Majesty King George II, whom I acknowledge as the sovereign lord of Acadia or Nova Scotia, so help me God."

All the Acadians needed to do was swear this oath—and the British would leave them alone. By 1730, the British had governed Acadia—which they called Nova Scotia—for nearly twenty years, but they had not been able to convince the Acadians to take an oath of allegiance to Britain. Finally, the Acadians agreed to take a modified version of the oath, in which a phrase was added excusing them from having to fight for the British. The Acadians were still French, after all; if they had agreed to take the full oath, they feared the British would ask them to fight against their friends and relatives in New France.

A Nova Scotian settlement

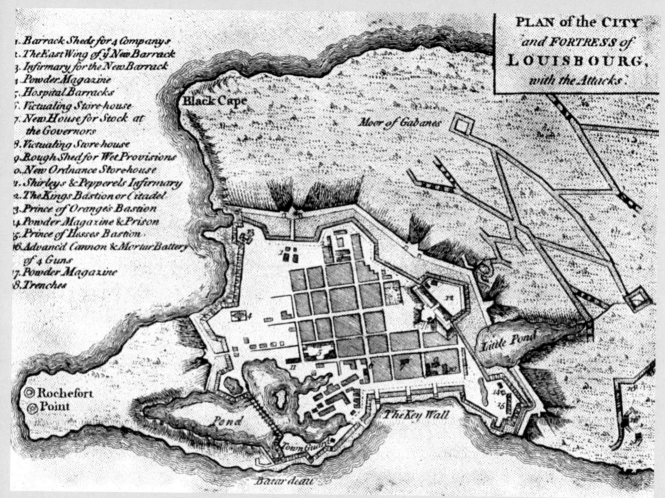

1. *Barrack Sheds for 4 Companys*
2. *The East Wing of ỹ New Barrack*
3. *Infirmary for the New Barrack*
4. *Powder Magazine*
5. *Hospital Barracks*
6. *Victualing Store-house*
7. *New House for Stock at the Governors*
8. *Victualing Store-house*
9. *Rough Shed for Wet Provisions*
10. *New Ordnance Storehouse*
11. *Shirleys & Pepperels Infirmary*
12. *The Kings Bastion or Citadel*
13. *Prince of Orange's Bastion*
14. *Powder Magazine & Prison*
15. *Prince of Hesses Bastion*
16. *Advanc'd Cannon & Mortur Battery of 4 Guns*
17. *Powder Magazine*
18. *Trenches*

PLAN of the CITY and FORTRESS of LOUISBOURG, with the Attacks.

Black Cape

Moor of Gabanes

Rochefort Point

Pond

Little Pond

Town Guard

The Key Wall

Batardeau

Map of the fort at Louisbourg

The Problem of Acadia

Acadia in the first half of the eighteenth century, after its conquest by the British, was usually a peaceful place. The Acadians farmed their land, worshipped in their Catholic churches, and kept on speaking French. Their numbers grew quickly, from less than two thousand in 1713, when British rule began, to around four thousand by 1730.

At first, the British gave the Acadians the opportunity to leave the area and relocate in Québec or another of New France's colonies. The Acadians did not want to abandon their land—the land they and their ancestors had worked so hard to settle.

As the Acadian population increased and kept refusing to take an unconditional oath of loyalty, the British started to get nervous.

The Acadians claimed to be neutral; they had promised not to take sides if a war began between Britain and France, but the British were not sure they could trust them. These French Acadians were a strong people, and there were now so many of them. If they left all at once, they could strengthen New France to the point where the French might decide to try and reclaim Acadia from the British. Even though the British had wanted the Acadians to leave in 1713, they soon decided they needed to keep them

Québec in the eighteenth century

where they were. If the Acadians left, it would be on British terms.

Louisbourg

When the British had taken control of Acadia in 1713, the French had kept the islands in the Gulf of St. Lawrence, including Île Royale—Cape Breton. The town of Louisbourg grew up on the eastern end of Île Royale at around the time of the British takeover. Most of the residents were fishermen who had left the French fishing villages on the south coast of Newfoundland when the Treaty of Utrecht had given their land to Britain.

In 1719, the French began to build a fortress in Louisbourg. The fortress would act as a base for French warships and would help protect the entrance of the St. Lawrence River from enemies. For twenty-six years, the French worked on the fortress and on fortifying the town of Louisbourg. They

built a wall to enclose the town and the fort, although they never completely finished the wall.

The British did not like the presence of Louisbourg so close to their own colonies. They worried the Acadians would leave Nova Scotia and travel to Île Royale. With so great a force at the Louisbourg fortress, the French might become truly dangerous.

King George's War

In 1744, Britain and France again went to war with each other in Europe, and as always, the fighting spilled over into North America. In North America, the war was called King George's War, the third of the French and Indian Wars.

France began the fighting in Canada with a series of attacks on British settlements in Nova Scotia. The French captured Canso, a little fishing village on the eastern end of British-held Acadia, just across from Île Royale. They also tried but failed to capture Annapolis Royal, which had been their Acadian capital Port Royal.

The British struck back with an attack on Louisbourg in the spring of 1745. The French in Louisbourg held out for nearly two months, but their great fortress—which had only just been completed after twenty-

A portrayal of a Mi'kmaq

The Mi'kmaq

Ever since the French had first settled in Acadia, back in the early 1600s, the Mi'kmaq had been their allies. By the time of the British takeover, the French and Mi'kmaq had been friends for over a hundred years. While the Acadians agreed to stay neutral in any fighting between the British and French, the Mi'kmaq made no such agreement. They stayed loyal to the French. For years, they launched attacks and raids on English settlements in Acadia. In fact, if the Acadians had agreed to pledge an unconditional oath of allegiance to Britain, the Mi'kmaq would have counted this an act of betrayal and might have turned on the Acadians as well.

six years of construction—did not live up to their expectations. The fortress was next to the harbor, with nearby hills rising above it from behind. The British discovered they could climb these hills and fire their cannons down into the fortress itself, instead of just firing at the walls.

Worse for the French was the situation inside Louisbourg. Only months before the British attack, in December 1744, a group of soldiers had *mutinied*, angry that they did not have enough food, enough clothing, or even enough firewood. The ill-kept soldiers, in their awkward fortress, could hardly turn back a concentrated British attack.

Mutinied means that soldiers or sailors refused to obey orders.

59

The attack on Louisbourg was the major British victory of the war. Thousands of young New Englanders had enlisted for the sole purpose of defeating the French at Louisbourg. For years they had been hearing stories about the massive French fort being built on Île Royale. Louisbourg had become an image of the French threat, and the more the stories were repeated, the larger and more powerful the fortress appeared.

On June 28, 1745, with the British surrounding Louisbourg on land and sea, the French surrendered. Under the terms of surrender, the inhabitants were allowed to return to France with their belongings unharmed. For the next three years, the British controlled Île Royale and the great fortress of Louisbourg.

In 1748, the war ended with the Treaty of Aix-la-Chapelle. The treaty returned Île Royale to the French, and in exchange the British received Madras in India. The New England colonists did not care about India; they had captured Louisbourg and now they were being told to give it back. To soothe the New Englanders, British Parliament paid them for the cost of the Louisbourg siege.

The Deportation of the Acadians

An uproar broke out in the church as soon as the orders were read. The Acadian men were on their feet, shouting at the British soldiers. As of that day, September 5, 1755, the orders read, the lands, houses, and livestock of the Acadian people were to be for-

The British sea attack against Louisbourg

feited to the British. The 418 men who had come to the church at Grand Pré to hear the announcement, as they had been ordered to do, were to be kept prisoner there until transport ships arrived to remove them and their families from Nova Scotia.

Although the Acadians had lived in Nova Scotia under British rule since 1713 and had promised to stay neutral in any conflict between Britain and France, the British were not satisfied. Again and again they tried to convince the Acadians to swear an unconditional oath of allegiance, promising to be loyal to Britain and Britain's king. The Acadians refused; they promised to be neutral, but they would not promise to fight for the British.

In 1754, war broke out once again between Britain and France, and the Acadians' promise of neutrality was no longer enough. The British did not trust the Acadians. They suspected them of secretly helping the French and the Mi'kmaq—longtime allies of the French—to plot attacks against British settlers. In 1755, the British tried once more to talk the Acadians into swearing the oath, and again the Acadians refused.

The lieutenant-governor of Nova Scotia, Charles Lawrence, decided the British needed to get rid of the Acadians. He worried that if the British simply exiled the settlers, they would go to Québec and help the French fight against the English. The Acadians numbered nearly ten thousand, and their presence would greatly strengthen the French's position in North America.

Halifax in the eighteenth century

Halifax

After the British returned Louisbourg to the French in 1748, they decided they needed to build a fortress of their own in Nova Scotia. This fortress would be the capital of Nova Scotia, replacing Annapolis Royal, and would defend against any threats from the French in Louisbourg. In 1749, the British chose Chebucto harbor, on the south side of Nova Scotia, in which to build their new capital. In June of the same year, sixteen ships arrived in Chebucto carrying 2,500 settlers. The British named their new city Halifax in honor of Lord Halifax, the president of the Board of Trade, who encouraged the establishment of the settlement. Halifax was the first British-founded town in Nova Scotia and soon became a busy seaport.

The Acadian men hearing the orders of deportation

Instead of just telling the Acadians to leave, Lawrence wrote orders to his men, telling them to *deport* the Acadians and scatter them throughout the British North American colonies.

The deportation of the Acadians began on September 5, 1755, and continued for the next several years. Families were herded onto transport ships; they were allowed to take with them only the few belongings they could carry. The British soldiers burned fields and houses so the Acadians would have nothing to come back to if they escaped.

Nearly ten thousand Acadians were uprooted from their homes and dropped off at British colonies along the coast of North America. Many ended up in Louisiana, where they became known as Cajuns. The British carried out the deportation of the Acadians because they were at war, and they considered the Acadians a threat to their safety. They believed they were justified in their actions, but for the thousands of Acadians whose lives were changed forever, the tragedy was overwhelming.

From the beginning of their history, the Acadians found themselves in a hard position, caught between the French to their north and the British to their south. Inevitably, they faced frequent attacks as Britain and France fought war after war for control of the continent. British rule had given the Acadians decades of peace, but their refusal to give up their heritage and take an unconditional oath of allegiance to

The exile of Acadians

Britain was costly. The British did not trust the Acadians—these quiet, hardworking people who stubbornly insisted on staying neutral. The deportation of the Acadians was one of the greatest tragedies of Canadian history. Years would pass before the Acadians were allowed to return to their land. Thousands died in the meantime from disease or from starvation.

Having cleared Nova Scotia of the Acadians, the British brought in their own people to settle and work the land. The French had caused problems for the British in North America for over a century, and the British wanted to drive them out of New France for good. The last of the four French and Indian Wars, begun in 1754, would soon spread to Québec, where the British would battle for control of the continent.

To **deport** someone means to expel or banish him from his own country.

65

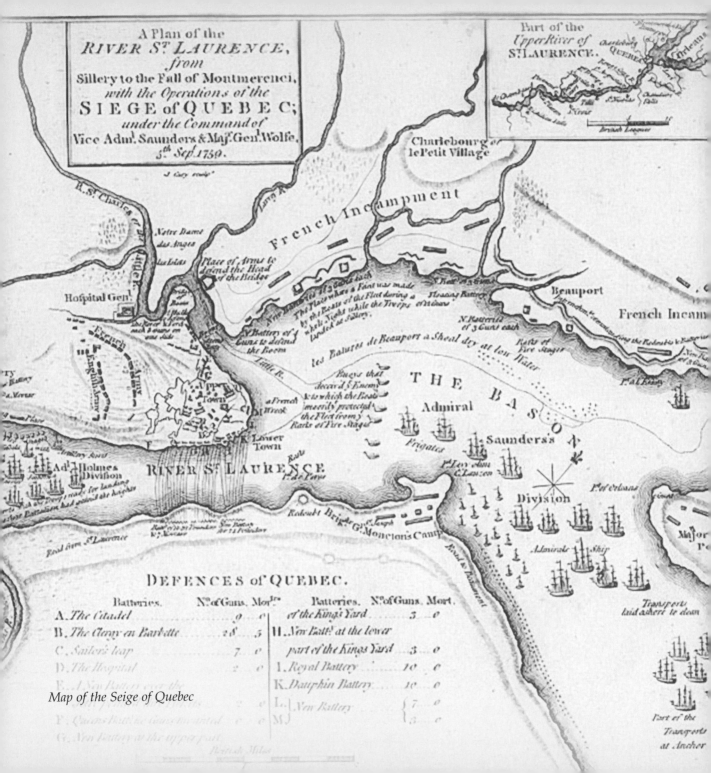

A Plan of the
RIVER St. LAURENCE,
from
Sillery to the Fall of Montmorenci,
with the Operations of the
SIEGE of QUEBEC;
under the Command of
Vice Adml. Saunders & Majr. Genl. Wolfe.
5th Sep. 1759.

Part of the
Upper River of
St. LAURENCE.

Charlebourg or
le Petit Village

French Incampment

French Incamp.

Beauport

R. St. Charles or

Notre Dame
des Anges

les Islets

Hospital Genl.

Place of Arms to
defend the Head
of the Bridge

N. Battery of 4
Guns to defend
the Boom

les Batures de Beauport a Shoal dry at low Water

N. Battery
of 3 Guns each

Floating Battery

N. Battery
of 3 Guns each

Rafts of
Fire Stages

THE BASON

Admiral

Frigates

Saunders's

Pt. Levi and
C. Lauzon

Division

Pt. d'Orleans

Town

Lower
Town

RIVER St. LAURENCE

Adml. Holmes
Division

Redoubt

Brigr. Gl. Monctons Camp

Road to Richmond

Admirals Ship

Major P.

Transports
laid ashore to clean

DEFENCES of QUEBEC.

Batteries.	No. of Guns.	Mortrs.	Batteries.	No. of Guns.	Mort.
A. The Citadel	9	0	of the King's Yard	3	0
B. The Clergy en Barbette	28	5	H. New Batty. at the lower		
C. Sailor's leap	7	0	part of the Kings Yard	3	0
D. The Hospital	2	0	I. Royal Battery	10	0
E. A New Battery over the			K. Dauphin Battery	10	0
F. Queens Battie. Guns mounted	0	0	L. New Battery	{ 7	0
G. New Battery at the upper part			M.	{ 3	0

British Miles

Part of the
Transports
at Anchor

Six

THE END OF NEW FRANCE

Red streaks had begun to spread across the eastern sky as hundreds of small boats rowed quietly toward shore. Through the early morning sea fog, the British soldiers in the boats could just make out the hills ahead of them in the gray predawn light. The great French fortress of Louisbourg was off to their northeast, but this beach was the only possible landing place for the British troops. It was too quiet, the soldiers thought. They knew the French were on the shore ahead of them—somewhere.

The attack came suddenly, guns and cannons firing from the shore. Many of the boats were hit and started taking in water. "Retreat!" shouted the commander, James Wolfe, and the little boats turned back to sea.

As the British landing craft moved away from the beach, several were swept to one side, into a little alcove of rock. The men in these boats realized they were sheltered from the French guns in their current position. Above them, they saw one of the French cannons. The French soldiers had not yet noticed them. Quietly, the British soldiers crept up the rocks toward the cannon.

Wolfe, looking back, saw what had happened. He signaled his men, and they rowed toward the alcove of rock. This was all the opportunity the British needed. Before the sun had fully risen over the horizon, the British had captured the beach, and the French soldiers had fled back to Louisbourg. With a foothold on Île Royale, the British knew it was only a matter of time before Louisbourg would fall.

The attack by Wolfe on Québec

The French and Indian War

The fourth and last of the French and Indian Wars—called simply the French and Indian War—broke out in 1754. At first the fighting was mainly restricted to frontier forts in New York and Pennsylvania. In 1756, fighting began in Europe as well, known there as the Seven Years' War.

Until 1758, the outcome of the war wavered back and forth. Then, Sir William Pitt, a British secretary of state, took charge of the war and things began to move in Britain's favor.

First came the victory over Louisbourg in July. As soon as the British had control of the fort, they demolished it in case they might have to give it back to France at the end of the war, as they had in 1748. Over the next several months, Fort Frontenac, at the eastern end of Lake Ontario, and Fort

Duquesne, near present-day Pittsburgh, Pennsylvania, both fell to British forces.

The Plains of Abraham

In the summer of 1759, Britain launched a major assault against Québec City, the capital of New France. General James Wolfe, who had helped secure the victory at Louisbourg, commanded the British forces.

The French did not think the British would be able to take the city, since it was built high on rocky cliffs. They did not even believe the British cannons could shoot far enough to hit the walls. They were wrong. Two hundred British ships sailed up the St. Lawrence River late in June and quickly captured the hills across the river from the city. From there, they began a long bombardment of the city with their cannons, while General Wolfe worked on a better way to attack.

Wolfe was a young man, only thirty-two at the time of the siege of Québec. He was tall and thin and had been sickly all his life. He made rash decisions and was moody and hard to get along with. His men thought he must be crazy.

The frustration of waiting out a siege quickly irritated Wolfe. He took out his anger on the countryside of New France by

James Wolfe

sending men to burn houses and fields and to slaughter livestock. He knew winters came quickly in Canada; if he did not take Québec by the time snow began to fall, he would have to retreat until spring. In the

70

winter, his ships would freeze into the ice of the river and be at the mercy of the French.

Before General Wolfe could give up, however, he discovered a path leading up through the 170-foot (52-meter) cliffs from the river to the Plains of Abraham, the plateau next to the city. The British soldiers crept up the path, calling out in French to the sentries, pretending they were bringing supplies for the city.

On the morning of September 13, over five thousand British soldiers waited on the Plains of Abraham. Louis-Joseph de Montcalm, the French general, had not expected an attack from that side of the city. Although he had been cautious with his

The death of Wolfe

troops up to this point, he feared the British would soon bring in even more soldiers. He and about 6,500 men marched out of the city to meet them on the plain.

The British had come with well-trained soldiers, experienced and well equipped. Most of Montcalm's men, on the other hand, had no experience with battles. They had been facing the constant barrage of British cannons for months, and their morale was low.

The battle lasted only half an hour. The first French charge broke and scattered into disorganized chaos. Montcalm could not rally his men enough to make another strong charge and was forced to retreat to the city. In the retreat, he was fatally wounded.

General Wolfe had also been fatally wounded during the fighting. He lived just long enough to learn the British had won the battle.

Five days later, on September 18, the French surrendered the city of Québec. The main stronghold of New France had fallen to the British.

The French in St. John's

The French had lost all their Canadian territory, but that did not mean they had completely given up. In the spring of 1762, France launched an attack against St. John's, Newfoundland, a major British port. They quickly captured the city and began raiding the surrounding communities. In September, British forces arrived to take back their city. The French surrendered on September 18, 1762, after a day of fighting. This was the final battle of the French and Indian War.

The Battle of Montréal

With the fall of Québec City, New France was nearly defeated. The remaining Canadian forces retreated to Montréal, up-river from Québec. At first, the British did nothing. They pulled back and waited for spring. The British forces left at Québec City shivered miserably in the remains of the city; the two-month British bombardment had left it in ruins.

In the summer of 1760, the British moved on Montréal to finish the French. Three separate British forces marched toward the city, one from Québec City in the east, one from the Great Lakes in the west, and one from Lake Champlain in the south. Altogether, 17,000 British troops converged on the last fortress of New France. The French waited with only two thousand men.

The French commander, François Gaston de Lévis, wanted to fight the British to the death, but the governor disagreed. On September 8, 1760, the French surrendered Montréal. The British now controlled Canada.

The Royal Proclamation made Murray governor, replacing the British military government.

The End of the War

On February 10, 1763, the French and Indian War—and the Seven Years' War in Europe— officially ended. France gave up any claims to its former Canadian territory in Acadia and along the St. Lawrence River. Instead, France received back the island of Guadeloupe in the Caribbean, which they wanted for its sugar crops. In Canada, France was only able to keep the tiny islands of St. Pierre and Miquelon, off the south coast of Newfoundland. These islands are still part of France.

The long series of French and Indian Wars was over with the fall of New France. With this threat gone, Britain issued the Royal Proclamation of 1763. The proclamation forbade any settlement west of the Appalachian Mountains and gave this land to the Native people. The British hoped to end the violent frontier warfare that had taken place during the wars with the French. The Royal Proclamation upset many American colonists and contributed to their growing desire for freedom from Britain.

Pontiac's Rebellion

Although the French had surrendered Canada to the British, some of their First Nations allies had not given up. They feared the British would try to enslave them. While the French had treated them as equals, the British seemed to look down on them as inferior.

Pontiac's Rebellion

Pontiac, a chief of an Ottawa tribe, led an unsuccessful attack on Fort Detroit in April of 1763. From this followed a series of First Nations uprisings against the British. Many British frontier forts were captured in these attacks. In 1764, the British struck back, cutting the First Nations off from their supplies of ammunition. Still, another two years passed before Pontiac finally surrendered.

The Royal Proclamation of 1763, issued after the Pontiac Rebellion had begun, was partly a response to this First Nations uprising. The British hoped Pontiac and his allies would be satisfied with a restriction on western settlement. As it was, most settlers ignored the proclamation. Many already lived in the restricted areas—the entire St. Lawrence region was west of the line, for example—and had no intention of leaving. The wars with the Natives the British had hoped to avoid would continue for the next century and a half, as settlers relentlessly pushed further west.

The Acadians Come Back

In 1764, with the war over and New France defeated, the British cancelled the orders exiling the Acadian people from their homes. By now, the Acadians had been scattered; many of them had died during the deportation.

Slowly, some began to make their way back to Acadia. Of the ten thousand who had been transported out of Nova Scotia, around three thousand returned. They had come home, but their old lives were gone forever. They had left established farms on some of the best farmland in Canada. The British had burned their barns and houses and brought in British settlers to live on their land. The Acadians could not simply pick up where they had left off.

Prince Edward Island

The Acadians moved north of their former land, to the coasts of New Brunswick. There they settled, most becoming fishermen. They swore allegiance to Britain, as they had earlier refused to do. They had survived great hardships, but they *had* survived. Today, the Acadians still live in parts of New Brunswick and Nova Scotia.

The British had won the war against France in North America. Their conflict had gone on since the discovery of the New World, but now Britain ruled the continent. The conquest of New France would soon cause problems for Great Britain, however. Without the distracting tension of the French and Indian Wars, the New England colonies realized how dissatisfied they were becoming with British rule. Grumblings began, hints of the revolution to come.

In Canada, the British faced the challenge of governing a large group of French-speaking people alongside a large group of English-speaking people.

Over the next hundred years, the Canadians would begin exploring westward. Canada would become a country.

Prince Edward Island

After the French left Canada, Prince Edward Island—then called St. John's Island—was left nearly deserted. Between 1764 and 1766, the British surveyed the land and divided it up into lots. Then, in 1767, the lots were auctioned off to landlords who would sign up settlers. The settlers cleared the land and paid rents to the landlords. In 1798, the island's name was changed to Prince Edward Island.

1534 Jacques Cartier claims the St. Lawrence River region for France.

1613 Samuel Argall is sent by Jamestown to rid the French from "English" territories.

1497 John Cabot claims east coast of North America for England.

1583 Sir Humphrey Gilbert claims Newfoundland for England and establishes St. John's.

1530s Church of England breaks away from the Catholic Church.

1607 England establishes colony on the east coast of Newfoundland.

1610 Henry Hudson explores Hudson Bay.

August 1610 John Guy and colonists establish Cupids, Newfoundland.

1629 Champlain surrenders the colony of Québec to the English.

1621 George Calvert establishes Ferryland, Newfoundland.

1638 David Kirke becomes the first governor of Newfoundland.

1621 Sir William Alexander establishes New Scotland— Nova Scotia.

1632 France regains control of New France.

1649 King Charles is beheaded.

1628 England sends the Kirke brothers to drive the French out of Canada.

79

1688 King William's War begins; war ends in 1697 with the Treaty of Ryswick.

1713 British take control of Acadia.

May 2, 1670 King Charles II grants Hudson's Bay Company a trade monopoly.

1690 Sir William Phips sent to take over Acadian settlements and to attack Québec.

1682 The French form La Compagnie du Nord to compete with Hudson's Bay Company.

1702 Queen Anne's War (Spanish War of Succession) begins; war ends in 1713 with Treaty of Utrecht.

1707 Parliaments of England and Scotland join to create the Parliament of Great Britain.

1754 French and Indian War (Seven Years' War) begins.

1829 Last of the Beothuks dies.

1744 King George's War begins; war ends in 1748 with Treaty of Aix-la-Chapelle.

September 8, 1760 French surrender Montréal, giving British control of Canada.

June 28, 1745 French surrender Louisbourg to the British.

1763 British issue the Royal Proclamation of 1763.

1749 British establish Halifax.

September 5, 1755 British order deportation of Acadians; order was cancelled in 1764.

FURTHER READING

Ferry, Steven. *Quebec*. San Diego, Calif.: Lucent Books, 2003.

Green, Carl P. *The French and Indian War*. Berkley Heights, N.J.: MyReportLinks.com Books, 2002.

Henty, G. A. *With Wolfe in Canada: The Winning of a Continent*. Mill Hall, Pa.: PrestonSpeed Publications, 2000.

Hibbert, Christopher. *Wolfe at Quebec*. Cleveland, Ohio: World Publishing Company, 1959.

LeVert, Suzanne. *New Brunswick*. New York: Chelsea House, 2000.

Mahaffie, Charles D., Jr. *A Land of Discord Always: Acadia from Its Beginnings to the Expulsion of Its People, 1604–1755*. Camden, Maine: Down East Books, 1995.

Marrin, Albert. *Struggle for a Continent: The French and Indian Wars, 1690–1760*. New York: Atheneum, 1987.

Mason, F. Van Wyck. *The Battle for Quebec*. Boston: North Star Books, 1965.

Russell, Francis. *The French and Indian Wars*. New York: American Heritage Publishing Company, 1962.

Smith, Carter, ed. *Battles in a New Land*. Brookfield, Conn.: Millbrook Press, 1991.

Tallant, Robert. *Evangeline and the Acadians*. New York: Landmark Books, 1957.

Wartik, Nancy. *The French Canadians*. New York: Chelsea House, 1989.

FOR MORE INFORMATION

Acadian History
www.girouard.org/
cgi-bin/page.pl?file=Ahistory&n=9

The Beothuk
www.heritage.nf.ca/aboriginal/
beothuk.html

Blupete, History of Acadia
www.blupete.com/Hist/NovaScotiaBk1/
TOC.htm

The Colony of Avalon
www.heritage.nf.ca/avalon/history/
default.html

Exploration and Settlement:
Newfoundland and Labrador Heritage
www.heritage.nf.ca/exploration/
default.html

Fort Anne, Annapolis Royal
www.pc.gc.ca/lhn-nhs/ns/fortanne/
index_e.asp

The Fortress of Louisbourg
collections.ic.gc.ca/louisbourg/
enghome.html

The French and Indian War
www.u-s-history.com/pages/h608.html

The History of Halifax
www.mikecampbell.net/
harbourvisitors.htm

Hudson's Bay Company History
www.hbc.com/hbcheritage/history

The Plains of Abraham
www.ccbn-nbc.gc.ca/_en/
batailles.php?section=1

Publisher's note:
The Web sites listed on this page were active at the time of publication. The publisher is not responsible for Web sites that have changed their addresses or discontinued operation since the date of publication. The publisher will review and update the Web-site list upon each reprint.

INDEX

PICTURE CREDITS

Centre for Newfoundland Studies Archives: p. 26

Corel: pp. 36–37

Frederic Remington: p. 40

Library of Congress: pp. 47 (bottom left), 68–69

National Archives of Canada: pp. 10, 11, 18–19, 41, 44–45, 56–57, 60–61, 62–63, 64, 65

National Archives of Quebec: p. 46

National Library of Canada: pp. 28, 29, 43

Photos.com: pp. 14–15, 20–21, 22, 24–25, 34, 47 (right), 50, 53, 54, 76–77

Provincial Archives of Manitoba: p. 39

Yale University Library: p. 13

BIOGRAPHIES

Sheila Nelson was born in Newfoundland. She has written a number of history books for kids and always enjoys the chance to keep learning. She recently earned a master's degree and now lives in Rochester, New York, with her husband and daughter.

SERIES CONSULTANT

Dr. David Bercuson is the Director of the Centre for Military and Strategic Studies at the University of Calgary. His writings on modern Canadian politics, Canadian defense and foreign policy, and Canadian military, among other topics, have appeared in academic and popular publications. Dr. Bercuson is the author, coauthor, or editor of more than thirty books, including *Confrontation at Winnipeg: Labour, Industrial Relations, and the General Strike* (1990), *Colonies: Canada to 1867* (1992), *Maple Leaf Against the Axis, Canada's Second World War* (1995), and *Christmas in Washington: Roosevelt and Churchill Forge the Alliance* (2005). He has also served as historical consultant for several film and television projects, and provided political commentary for CBC radio and television and CTV television. In 1989, Dr. Bercuson was elected a fellow of the Royal Society of Canada. In 2004, Dr. Bercuson received the Vimy Award, sponsored by the Conference of Defence Association Institute, in recognition of his significant contributions to Canada's defense and the preservation of the Canadian democratic principles.